Beauty is a Liar

Valerie Joy Kalynchuk

Beauty is a Liar
© 2006 Valerie Joy Kalynchuk

Edited and designed by Andy Brown
First Edition
METRO SERIES

Library and Archives Canada Cataloguing in Publication

Kalynchuk, Valerie Joy, 1975-
    Beauty is a liar / Valerie Joy Kalynchuk.
ISBN 1-894994-15-9
    I. Title.
PS8571.A4155B43 2006   C813'.6   C2006-901637-2

Dépot Legal, Bibliothèque nationale du Québec
Printed in Quebec on 100% recycled, ancient rainforest
friendly paper.

Excerpts from *Beauty is a Liar* have previously appeared in:
Event and *Matrix*.

CONUNDRUM PRESS
PO Box 55003, CSP Fairmount,
Montreal, Quebec, H2T 3E2, Canada
conpress@ican.net   www.conundrumpress.com

conundrum press acknowledges the financial assistance of the
Canada Council for the Arts toward their publishing program.

Canada Council   Conseil des Arts
for the Arts   du Canada

Beauty is a Liar

Valerie Joy Kalynchuk

"Truth is beautiful, without a doubt.
But so are lies."

—Ralph Waldo Emerson

conundrum press
Montreal

Dlia miy bat'ko

(For my father)

There are five of us in my grandpa's car. My grandma sits in the passenger's seat, my mother behind her. Layla, the girl my mother babysits, and whom I guess is also my friend, is in between us. I press my forehead to the window, under the pretense of not wanting to miss the hefty cows who are huddled together in the rain, or the thin horses who seem not to want to bother with each other. In truth I am trying to hide the fact that I can't look like I've had a pleasant day. I am grateful for the sheeting rain, and for the hard cool window, a relief after the pounding hot afternoon. When my mother points out more farm animals on her side, she's happy for Layla's unfeigned enthusiasm over the nodding sheep, since to her I seem as if I don't care. I pretend to look, but only sideways. If she sees the look cut into my face she will either say nothing about it or else half-smile and push her glasses up on her nose to snap, "Why do you look so miserable anyway?" I don't know. If I begin to cry, which I feel like I might, I guess I could claim it is all the ragweed on the roadside, or maybe the fact that my grandpa's every orifice seems to exude a pungent raw sliced onion odour, but of course I can't say the latter.

We have come from the Morden Corn and Apple Festival. My grandparents like to go to these Manitoba summer country fairs where the midways consist of those air filled structures you enter, a gigantic clown head or Garfield mouth, and the game in which you bash down balls with a big foam mallet to win a stuffed turquoise elephant, or more than likely a New Kids On The Block sticker. Layla had dragged me into the clown mouth today but I only sidled to a corner and tried to keep from falling over with all the bouncing on the trapped ersatz air. Of course there were the requisite cobs of corn and dixie cups of apple cider, but there were also apple pan dowdy on toothpicks, and whole apple pies latticed with pastry the consistency of cardboard. My grandpa told my grandma, "No one makes as good a pie crust as you do Mum." There were also small corn fritters which bled grease onto the Morden Chamber of Commerce napkins. There were candy apples which somehow got stuck in my hair even though it was slicked back into a ponytail. Miss Morden Corn and Apple 1983 threaded through the crowd, her mouth frozen in a shiny large-toothed Vaseline smile, her head about to topple over because of the crown of apples, corn, and sprigs of golden canola.

Now the acres of canola we pass are blunted and defeated against the wind and rain, and somehow greyish. Violet and black clouds on the prairie horizon promise more powerful storms, and I hope for cracking lightning before we reach the city limits. There is nothing like a prairie thunderstorm, and years later when I will leave this place and hem and haw back and forth between coasts, these storms will be the only things I miss.

Layla and I seem to be the only ones in the car who aren't growing anxious by the storm. My grandpa keeps clearing his throat and reaching for a handkerchief, spitting his tobacco hack into it instead of opening the window. I can see my grandma wring her hands, and when I turn my head to look at my mother she is gripping the handle on the door. Both my mother and my grandma have hands that always appear to have a sheen of oil on them, and protruding veins, as if they have been kneading Criscoed dough all day long.

The sky finally cracks and splits with forked lightning, and I wish I could run from the car and lie in the field, caressed by the violence of the sky. Layla places a deck of cards on top of two Archie comics in the little space between our laps and nudges me. "Wanna play go fish?" I shake my head no, and get ready to tune out my mother's sing song, "Uh oh... go fish!"

It rains harder yet. I am no longer frowning, and a thrill rushes through me with each roll of thunder, with each press of lightning breaking the sky in two. It hails for a few minutes, ice pummeling the car like a rain of bullets. Most of the fields seem to be alone, there are few farm houses seen from the road, and I try not to think of what the devastation will do to the people who have tended the wheat and canola and alfalfa. The animals are taking the storm in stride. The cattle are aware of their slaughterhouse fate, and probably wish they could be struck down now by nature.

As we get closer to the outskirts of the city my heart sinks as I see the sun melting through the clouds. "Oh thank God," my grandma says. I would rather ask Why God, because this summer the city has had virtually no rain, no storms such as these, and I know there will be endless sun drenched days when my mother will harangue me to go play outside with Layla, and I will be forced to go with them all next week to the Carmen Country Fair, and stop and eat chicken at seedy looking truck stops with waitresses who will tell me I'm cute in the pink ribbon barrettes my mother uses to pull back my hair.

Sunshine is more portentous to me than black clouds about to burst. Sunshine with its cheer as false as the school guidance counselor when she calls you in to tell you you are not motivated enough to go into AP English when you get to grade seven three years from now. Sunshine is a spirit I no longer have, if I ever had it at all. Sunshine is a let down day whenever I wake up and am forced to face it. Even slathered up in SPF 45 I end up lobster red. Rain and the sky clouded over is what I am, void of any wish. I do not feel I am anything but moving along, lying in wait for something I cannot see, but expect when my grandpa asks my mother every fall, "Why doesn't she get off her ass and rake the leaves?" Every season brings a new failing and if it were possible I'd rather stay where the weather is the same, the weather I can appreciate. Sun makes you squint at the glinting plastic silver of Layla's jacks, sunlight takes all the mystery out of stained glass windows, sunshine makes you expect things that never happen. In the winter it makes you think there are diamonds in the snow, but when you touch them they melt away to nothing.

I want only storm eyes, careening spiraling tornadoes, I want my grandpa's neck to tense as he is driving down the highway. I want AM talk radio programs about the benefits of mega dose vitamin C to be pre-empted by extreme weather warnings. I do not want sun showers or starlight. I want torrential downpours and gale gust winds. I want umbrellas to be outlawed. People have humility when they are drenched. I want to run out in the inclement and wear the same soaked clothes the next day, and the day after that, smelling of musty dried rain. I want to be late for school every day because the bus broke down in a street river. I want my mother's tomatoes to get too much water and fall over under the weight of it. I want the rain to be layered and go two directions at once. I want the lightning to strike the house and the power to go out so I can look out of my bedroom window while the rest of them cower in the basement.

But there is the Richardson building. Portage and Main, the corner you have to pass to get anywhere within the city, and far away from it. It's not raining. Not even spitting. The sun off the few office building mirrored windows will trick birds into thinking they are flying further, and the impact of the sky reflected will stun them out of their flight to the heated ground below. When we get home I will have to play outside with Layla in the bushes that will leave us covered in inching canker worms. Then I will have to eat bright yellow corn on the cob, and make everyone think I am making my candy apple last because I like the sweet and sticky. I do know now why I was verging on tearful. It was not of envy of them liking Layla better, it was not my grandparents and my mother looking above my head all day. It was envy of the horses and longing to stand in the centre of an empty field during a vicious storm. I don't want lazy summer days browning down my skin after the burn peels away. I want wild unforgiving weather. I want to dance languid in an expanse of land flooded and never to be drained of driving rain, and wind that is not a cautious spring breeze. I do not want to laugh or cry again. I want to breathe the air made clean, the rains never to stop. I want to be solid and steady on the muddy ground and the sky made passionate by gods out-numbering one.

Lord Wall I don't remember it but you walked me in circles in my colic soliloquies while spinning your algebraic monologues. I still cannot add single digits without counting on my fingers. You would lace yours together palms outward because you were the genus genius, the genesis. You proved the white coats wrong when blue chested men showed up at our door with guns drawn, and your rifle was your tongue and left them tongue tied. There was always a camera eye through the one skylight you always had to have the tin cans lined up in the cupboard right. I check doors are locked fires are out wallet is in my pocket getting into taxi cabs. When I had the chance to meet you for the first time again would I have been Snow White or a cocker spaniel because the Disney people were making a movie about your life. And when I'm in the café and the lady screaming passes by and they all laugh or look away it's you on an Eastside Vancouver street, your tattered cloak in the wind of your preaching. So I give coins to bums so that maybe you'll eat or consider living somewhere other than behind the supermarket that sells everything from clam chowder to fuchsia tank tops but I know you won't. Your course has always been the off course vernacular of the chorus within. You would have been disappointed if my early cries turned to what you would understand as being passionate apathy. You would forever heed your virus just as your own father stood still to die on the prairie in a ring of fire. Was that when you so blissfully fell from grace or to the grace so graced. When I was born you wanted to dip your Dali brush into my placenta coil stroke my birth right your curse blessing. Yes your rhapsodies let me dance dance to the feedback and high and low whisperings. To be apprehensive of nothing you would have me be never apprehended for who I could become who I already was who was that. But I did not go and see you and could only absorb your signals to me in the not so cryptic messages on the sides of city buses, the street lamps going off one by one as I argued with a good friend. You will always be Lord Wall, carving your staff out of cork with a thin paring knife. You will always be one who I will. One I feel I must fold over in honour, but I still don't speak up at those every second day crazy people jokes told. I will just seethe. Who really are the mad ones. You wouldn't mind however. You'd tell them they were right, right? "Embrace," you'd hiss and they'd think for a moment you were telling them to have a group hug and they'd be uncomfortable thinking they'd have to touch you too, and you'd laugh knowing you were both Einstein and Eisenstein editing your equations. If they realized this they'd all be reaching out and tugging at your clothes. You wore wine red during the week and black on

Sundays. Sleep was for the weak and so were mansions and hovels. So was trying something new to eat. And then every day the same thing for months. I have done this too I guess, so have a lot of people. I do love my most intimate stranger whose eyes are a shock to meet every morning in the mirror. Sure there are shadows there and wailing light too. Everyone at one time or another has had to wait to pass through doors with loud buzzers to doubt what is supposed to be real, to create things, to do things no one else understands. Everyone has talked too fast, avoided responsibility, wanted someone to listen or simply sit with them. But you were singled out shooed away hypodermics and four point restraints. A life lived without a calendar. You could tell it was Christmas when there was no one on the streets. When you saw that the daylight was going on and on into evening. And that one day there was a new kind of perceiving, one just as brilliant in sight and sound as the one of your whole life. You had wonder of that light and said, Well now isn't that something, and the stranger you remarked this to didn't turn away and after the longest day was through you finally stepped away. You bequeath me your staff and I see through my own eyes gradients in every colour as endless as π. Say goodnight to third birthday feather cake and the train to snow lake and say what do you mean when people say how about this crazy weather. And that wailing light of yours nailed to water burst sky. One extra candle for the mystery for the heart for my ungoodbye.

Ice on feathers. Layers bold in blue. We shook from the night terrors. Awoke safe and sound in the sounds of the solace of spring. I do not want to look at or wear things she has given me. I give them away. When things frighten me I think how much more frightened are you knowing that I know the truth. You were given life and chose to hurt my heaven. Memory serves me right. You are the one who causes winter to come. Satiated with this wisdom. My mouth no longer seeks out your breast.

She is not ninth she is negative one and I am ill that we shared a body. So the bright blinding words say kill it. So I falter in my honesty. I do not like looking around. I do not like seeing. If I were blind it would be as the blue divine. Sacred divide. No we did not share a body. I came from the sky in perfect disguise. Tears tear holes and the wear shows my age. Shadow bruises sky blue now don't worry I will do it for you.

Your misery passed to me through our placenta and even then I was with watchful eyes waiting for the moon to tell me when to be born. I have held the knife so long that when I set it down the handle stays warm for a long time. Twice in my life you have embraced me. Time is empty. There is a cure for me in my wild moods but this makes either me or others turn away.

You are not alive slave to the slime. You are not alive ribbons for eyes. You are not alive I will scream at the mirror but I don't look like you. My feet are immersed in so cold water my hands in water so hot. You are not alive my dreams are bleeding creases. Tulips and waltz. I am not growing up I am growing up. You are not alive the clouds are no longer shy. You are not alive all your songs are streaming backwards. I like the way it sounds. It does not scare me anymore. I am night spotting planets. You are not alive the green is not grime.

You ran through the sixties chalking a circle in front of the old mansion built long ago by the man who stole the railway. In the circle it said, everything's okay in here, and the rain didn't wash it away. But then of course maintenance came and took quick care of it. Sometimes the rest of us wished we could feel your wind for ourselves. What it must have been like to make everyone around you smile and laugh. But we knew too that there would be a time, never knowing when, but you'd sit still like us so drawn and sober with that broken zipper over the eyes. And I prayed, squeezed those eyes, it would be a long time before the rest of us would be in the burnt umber of sabotaged friendships. Denial of every appetite we sideways glanced at the swirling pictures you taped up in the nicotine stained yellow room. The room where we gathered every hour for the seven minutes of a cigarette, those pictures, the fuzzy sweatered college student who tried to decipher, having had no luck with your Rorschachs. But those were no Degas ballerinas leaning over with thin grace lovingly caressing their satin shine shoes, their toes ripped up and bleeding. To imagine that your pictures were your marathon. You were sprinting, accepting no ice water along the way, and you relished the stitch in your side. Your father kept offering you another cookie cutter wondering why his own refused to use his persuasiveness to speak for higher ups who were padding their bank accounts, refurbishing their wives. You couldn't understand why we walked with our heads down unless it was to find spare change. We'd wake up for a time to watch you, to try and let ourselves see your iridescent turquoise dome above one palm curved toward the sun, the other still gripping the piece of chalk. Your messages all over the city when you could slip away sometimes without anyone noticing. White coats probed but were afraid to touch your palette that it would forever stain their hands. What else is turquoise. Those of us with energy still to ask the question almost pleaded and you simply planted a peck on each of our cheeks and ran down the long narrow hall and you naming yourself blue that we could brighten ours too.

Deemed ancient with no gracious redemption he presses away Sunday sunshine drag scraping scuff soles from park bench to park bench under shade. Pining the months away. Cryptic cold ice stormed glitter trees encase the blacked out panic city. Denied now by children. He tunes out who he could miss, holds fast. He resigns himself to the dread of returning to his narrow room and his kettle which is always so slow to come to a boil.

Sometimes I need a break. Don't tell anybody where we live. Say that you live there. Sun Valley nice houses like the other kids. It's by the IGA, the man-made lake. You have fun there. Sometimes I need a break.

Let's all hold hands and make a square. The prairie light is cold-filtered through the dusty blinds. The daycare woman doesn't read right and every story time sounds like weary meanness. Maybe I protested, or worse corrected, chose blue and not yellow. Whatever it was after the third week I stopped the fists and that child after milk choke sobbing the lock clicked on the closet door and no more clock. Mistaken they were those grim women who hated children, could not stand what was bright or muted. Would never caress a tale to hide their stumbling over the words. Each day after that first time I would hold my breath until I was purple pearl red and get them to lock me in. The mop and pail sheetrock crumble dirty rainbow beach ball losing air. Grow to be a giant, stuck neck and shoulders in the cob-webbed crook of the ceiling.

Tattle tale. Your drop of a mind is but congealing tallow while mutter what is miles past ignorance. Why not make the all of your time in observation outside in instead of everyone you're telling on.

Slack-eyed under gin and seven rifling through trashings for your clip wings and your 97th second chance. Barter with the double boiler and top a lid on it. You would be a mother and a grandmother mending many a skinned knee if you could ever push through the white ribbon at the end of the marathon. In the advent of flames on a willow treed boulevard. Hocking the gravy train no more. Third foot to trip the stagger back to youth's lackadaisical stroll. How many ounces of gratitude, if any left at all. Still life heart beat held in your hand carved picture frames. The sun rises on the mourning of blame.

I was rushing off to dance class earlier than I had to because my mother had asked in the door-to-door Mormons. They were sitting at the table with her in their cheap track suits and ties. "This is my daughter," my mother said. "She is going to her ballet class." Mother's eyes were blank and depressed, but her lip curled as the young men appraised me like some prize calf at auction. One of the men looked like Michael Bolton. "She is sixteen," my mother offered them eagerly. They wanted her to sit down so they could all pray together. Other than falling out with the woman who used to take us to the Lutheran church in her maroon station wagon (over an ill-fated plate of date squares apparently) I did not know that my mother was so lapsed and disillusioned that she was now considering another bible entirely. Perhaps it was because she was in some kind of state of searching like the ladies on *Oprah*, but unlike them this searching did not cause her to start wearing drapes for clothing, or comb sand in a miniature zen rock garden with a tiny rake. Instead it seemed to make her permeate a tension that grew as slowly and pervasively as the black mold on the bathroom tiles. I fumbled continually through this, and every time I did something like forgetting to wipe down those bathroom tiles, which of course perpetuated that mold, she would shriek, "Everything is falling apart!" If I lost my bus pass, as I did too often, my mother would guess and tell me, "I know how you work you know." I was at a loss, and kept putting off writing to Oprah, who helped women toward happiness by paying to redo their bathrooms so they could soak in papaya-scented bubble baths surrounded by candles—but not too long of course, for this could lead to dry flaky skin.

The Mormon boys asked a third time, "Are you sure you wouldn't like to come pray too?" I told them I had to go. Years later I would wish I had told them I was a white witch. When I left I closed the door quietly and my strides to the bus stop were quick and too long for my legs.

The bus was empty so I wondered why the man with stringy hair sat down next to me. There were no single seats on the older buses. I could get up and move to another empty double, or sit down on the long bench across from the bored driver, but instead I stayed put and tried to follow my peculiar thought pattern, thinking about endangered species, and then all the odd animals of Australia, who had such an alien quality they might have indeed just dropped there from the tail of a comet flying from another planet. The man got off by the bar with the cherry-lemon-cherry machines, lascivious more now for possible pails of quarters.

I jump highest of anyone in my dance class, though I am not very good at turning. I cannot whip my head around to the elusive spot that never changes, that keeps the other girls from veering off their course from the corner. In the change room Layla was picking a muffin away to tiny grains. She stuck them to her fingertips and pressed them to her tongue. Her arms were of the requisite sylph sort, but her calves were rock hard. She wore combat boots when she was not on her toes. "Keep your wings in," our sometimes gentle ballet mistress was always telling her, flattening Layla's shoulder blades into her back like the relief of two final puzzle pieces.

The bus on the way home was packed, and I held my head, feigning dizziness to justify putting my large heavy bag next to me on the double seat. Two women in pastel and paisley winter coats and dueling perfumes discussed why my hair was slicked back into a bun.

"Maybe she is a Hutterite," the one drenched in lavender said.

"But they don't wear pants," considered the one wearing Luvs baby soft.

"Shh, she'll hear us."

"Naw, she doesn't understand a word we're saying."

When I got home there was a pocket-sized vinyl covered *Book of Mormon* on the kitchen table. My mother offered me roast beef and gravy.

"I'll just have potatoes. I can't really eat meat anymore."

"Jesus Christ!" mother bellowed, "I don't know what to bloody make anymore."

"I'll start cooking my own dinner then." I stepped off the cliff because my mother curled her lip once again and in her crackle voice, "Yeah right. You can't cook for yourself. You don't do anything around here. If I didn't cook for you you wouldn't eat at all. You're lucky you're not diabetic because you'd forget to take your insulin. You'd be god-damned dead."

My mother unfolded a TV tray and set down a plate of mashed potatoes and broccoli boiled so long it was grey.

"Fine. You don't want what I make. I don't know what the hell to do anymore. I guess I'll go do the dishes now seeing as no one else will do them around here. Or anything else for that matter." I was the only other person living there, except for the cat. She crooned to him and attempted to walk him on an orange and green plastic leash. The cat would only scuttle a few steps, and then lie on the ground growling with his ears back and his fur standing on end. It's nice she has his companionship though, the way he curls up at the end of her bed each night. I wasn't lonely at night because my thoughts were as loud as a prison cafeteria. Often I was thinking of the whole concept of gratitude, and was puzzled as to why I did not ever show it. It just seemed easier and more natural to be sullen or blank.

I turned on the television and tried to swallow as much of the potatoes and dejected broccoli as I could. I could taste the beef drippings in the gravy on my potatoes, and wished I had said I'd rather have them plain. *Little House on the Prairie* was on, and I watched the Ingalls family pitch fork hay and churn butter, and utter saccharin rationalizations for Mary's blindness. The Ingalls had faith, and although I could not convince myself that my own faith in something or other was tepid, my stomach churned up the lard gravy taste when I remembered the avarice eyes of the Mormon men. One of them wore a gold bracelet, the other a mother of pearl tie clip. This struck me as incongruent with their eighty-five dollar track suits.

I rose to take my plate to the kitchen and felt grateful for how tired and sore my muscles were. I knew I would dive into sleep as soon as I hit my pillow. I was thankful too that my mother was on the phone with her back turned. I furtively poured my glass of milk down the sink. My mother looked back at me as I turned on the water to wash the dishes, and with a dismissive wave of her hand mouthed the words, "Oh just leave them." She was obviously on the phone with someone who was not a relative because her voice was as buoyant as the Romper Room lady.

"Oh, she is working so hard. They have a show at Christmas. Yeah. And she is still doing really well in school."

This reminded me that I had homework to do, and as I plodded up the stairs to my room it occured to me that my mother did not mention the afternoon table praying and probably wouldn't mention it to whomever she was on the phone with, unless she felt like talking about how good looking and how nice the men were. I thought of the man on the bus, who was not good looking, and I bet not too nice. The memory of it felt like the Tylenol and codeine tablets my mother gave me the nights I couldn't sleep, and the cups of strong coffee the mornings I had trouble waking up. I slouched over my desk and opened my math text book to fractions. The hunching was unfamiliar and uncomfortable. I concentrated on the string at the top of my head. The one our ballet teacher reminded us of when we were not tall enough, or the golden light the modern teacher talked about while gesturing like an infomercial life coach in slow motion. My back was straight but I was conscious of my shoulder blades sticking out. I rotated my shoulders and relished the crunching and popping sound of my bones. I pushed them in and they fit as puzzle perfect as Layla's did when she was corrected. I reached to run my hand over my back. My wings were nicely hidden. No one could see them.

Slouching in straight backed chair denying overnight tall. Too quiet cousin hears the ominous before the omen. Everybody falls over sparkling pink wine. She leaves hers untouched white knuckled control seventies orange brown apartment urine suppers. Uncles take turns sitting next to her. She puts her old Coke bottle glasses back on.

That's the way I just corner eyed fingerprints on the steak knife blade. Grandma sat me up on the counter, I swung my legs, and it was roof joy while she held my wrists. Spat, cleaned my face. So long piece of evening. Even this high no way to tell from the window what is the season. Sky vibrates grey stasis. Who has plucked the buds. Leaves frost from each ghetto yard yellow tree allotted. Growing up no ravens but smaller blackbirds, more streetsmart, dodge tarmac oil rainbows that fell from the same sky they had flown. A joke for a shiny nickel piece of the nest. A quick quip cajole for my cut glass broach and the silver flask with one sour drop that seems it may never ache away from the lip.

The Lutheran church was on Glenway, flat and pointed, spireless. Verses cut out of felt. Eye level for the tall stained glass octagons and triangles. Don't make picture stories of what's inside *that* book. Translucent too much. They let in only a bit of sun when it wanted to come in. The incense tipped over into the room and around my head last week made clean by a white palm of baptismal cold water and a name with the other little lambs each cut out of felt black shingled parking lot, count seventeen silver cars. White per capita superstition. You guys get the Christmas hamper. No one else is supposed to know but they may as well print your names on the turkey. The mystery gift is better than the welfare cheerboard dusty Halloween candy and creamed corn. But still my gratitude comes through ground teeth and I know I hate my shame and I hate my candy store kid dreams and I feel so odd as the bath water turns grey and I wonder why I can sing the hymns which echo off the porcelain but could only mouth the words in the pew between the two plump poly-ester ladies.

Uncle Milty often talked about acquiring a boathouse in Tahiti. He wanted to live it up, he said, and he wanted to find a gentle woman who enjoyed playing gin rummy. Uncle Milty had been married six times. He showed up at my grandmother's house with rolls of two dollar bills, and when the bills were fazed out for toonie coins he lamented how heavy they made the insides of his suit jacket pockets. No one asked questions, and I thought this was how large amounts of money came, leafed together or rolled in plastic.

Uncle Milty took me to the race track one day, and when I picked Amber's Lark to show he gave me my seven dollar winnings with a wide grin, and toasted my Coke with his beer, spilling froth on his polka dot tie which was so long it touched the table.

"You got intuition little lady."

Uncle Milty believed in reincarnation. He told me he was once a blacksmith in 18th century Quebec, and suspected he was one of Napoleon's lovers.

"There's nothing wrong with my having been a lady. It helped me understand them better. They want you to ask how they are, and listen to how they are for a few hours. They like sweet smelling or sparkly presents. One day some guy is gonna be sweet to you, and if he's not I'll break his knees."

I asked him what or who he thought I might

have been. He told me he thought I was probably a female deer, and because I always had to be swaddled tightly when I was baby, that I probably died by drowning in a past life.

"A shy little doe, I'm certain. Your eyes are always so wide and black. And look how you still don't know how to swim at your fine age."

He told me the point of reincarnation was to try and stop making the same mistakes over and over. He said you make the same mistakes when you are a cockroach as when you are the queen of England. I asked how that could be possible and he told me we were all sentient beings.

"What's a sentient being?"

"That means knowing, cognizant... ach... it means every living thing makes mistakes and covers them up. Look how much I gamble, I'll be losing my shirt in this life and the next. Let's just hope I end up a tailor." He leaned back in his chair and gave a great belly laugh.

Uncle Milty also tried to teach me how to astrally project. "Before you go to sleep you relax your whole body and think on where you want to go. Then you end up in a place, a good place, and you fly through it. It's heaven on Earth, but it's not really Earth or heaven. You can meet up with me or whoever is astrally projecting that night. And if anyone gives you any trouble you can poof them away just like that. Some say if you get good enough you can make people poof away in real life." I found this appealing since I couldn't stand my math teacher.

We left the track with Uncle Milty having won five hundred smackers.

"Let's go to Crappy Tire and get you a new bike."

"It's okay. My old bike is fine."

"Hey, don't ever think you deserve less than the best. Money buys happiness, and that's all there is to it."

Uncle Milty gave me books on Buddhism and I knew that desire was a bad thing but when I asked him about it he told me, "That's a lot of hooey. You learn from these things but you make them suit your own needs. And you don't double cross anyone. Unless, of course, it is absolutely necessary. Take me, when I was a lowly roach I didn't tell the others where the bit of sponge cake was. I kept it for myself. And I survived. It's survival of the fittest. We're at battle little lady and don't you forget it." My Uncle had a strong psychic shield, and I felt it whenever I was with him. It surrounded me like a large cumulus cloud. I felt no one or nothing could harm me if I was with him. I knew I needed my own. The kids on the playground sometimes picked on me, and I often fantasized about my Uncle breaking their knees. He told me it was wrong to act on violent impulses unless you were under attack, and I knew I had a lot to learn. But I didn't feel weak when I was with him, my Uncle was an extension of me, I could be as strong as he was, I could make money furtively in my later years, and he promised to leave everything he had to me.

When he told me he was going to Tibet to hold audience with the Dalai Lama I was sad to see him go. He asked me if I had a question for The Great Man, and I couldn't really think of anything except the general whys of the universe. But he pressed me to come up with something and so I asked him to ask if it is okay to be small and never want to be more than quiet.

"Oh honey, I can answer you that myself. It's okay to be small, but never be quiet. Stand up for yourself. Remember I was a lowly roach, but I took what I could get. And now I'm here, making big bucks at what some would call shady dealings. But I'm happy. And we're allowed to be that honey."

I received a postcard of the Himalayas and a note saying that on his way back to Canada Uncle Milty was going to stop in Atlantic City. He gave a forwarding address. I had my mother take a picture of me on my new red bicycle and I sent it to him.

In the picture my back was straight and tall, and I was riding down the tree-lined street, just about to turn the corner into a neighbourhood I'd never been to before. Uncle Milty then sent me another postcard with nothing but a big exclamation point in black marker, and I realized I was finally on to something.

A long time for a rock to hide Diana in a Winnipeg flea bag bar lit down green three blocks away from affluence. Auntie turnstile croons the waiver don't mean nothing. Her signature in grade six bubble cursive. Uncle Milty signs a bewildered nervous scrawl. All of this for her paste on glimmer grin to get that sequined glower gown.

Scales on an instrument forced upon other kids were often given up for a wet soccer field. Necessary as the silver rose scales on a fish to be able to swim. But after a while taken for granted, and the water's so contaminated there could never be any adaptation. I tried to learn these scales on my violin, they rose and retreated on a straight central staircase. Anybody home went upstairs closed doors covered ears. I was to understand it must be wretched for them but for me it was safety. This standing in one place. Then letting it move on a little more quickly each time. In the summertime there were parking lot repairs being done outside and when I practiced at the same time the others called it my cat in pain. To me it was a perfect counter cadence to the orchestra of the machines and the impatient cursing joking voices of the men working.

I was not as eager to get through the scales as Layla was with her piano lessons, easily tiring of what she saw as nothing more than extrapolated theory which only took away from time spent on learning real pieces she called songs. I thought of how the body had a symphony soundtrack, but the little understood brain, and the less understood mind, sounded more like this wonderful mess of scratches from a young student of a difficult instrument. The sounds of the necessary destruc-

tion of the pavement outside, the destruction necessary to repair it. That kind of music was as gor-
geous to me as the steady beating of the heart, and
if really listened to, as absorbing and comforting
as an Escher drawing.

So I practiced in the basement when I was told to
please stop now, with the echo of the unfinished
room and the constant drip of the laundry sink
tap. I went to school and when the teacher's long
red nails accidentally scratched down the chalkboard, I did not wince as the others did, but tilt-
ed my head and hoped it may happen twice more
during the day, once with the radiator clanking at
the same time, and once the exact same moment
as the lunch bell. And on my recital day, whatever
song I played, I would not play it from behind a
fourth wall but close with the chairs screeching
across the floor. As throats could not politely sup-
press their coughs. Fretfully colicky babies as
impatient and angry as those road workers who
realized that they'd made a glaring mistake. The
work would need to be done all over again.

That house is an abscess. Sparrows passing through get lost trying to find the window way out. Lose their appetite, turn their heads, and cough. Stiff sea maid and master of the house servants, butchers with paring knives, a contract to remain tight lipped. Clues are in the mail box. The fishy luck blotto lotto lady and mate may consider they have half of it right, conclusions come to by accident, keep talking, after that some other point will spill out. This novelty for rotating the help every week wore down two bank accounts, cluck queries about assets, the dolled don't tell.

That house is flim flam. The tea rose water closet appreciating the notion of notions, to sew and going on that dole. They want to experience it all in a special vacation package. Rueful is so charming. Still swearing spouting oaths still love for white linens. Where the porpoises are dyed pink and the water's raspberry slush puppy blue for the grandchildren who are so thirsty and grow on the liquid soother and subdued glamour never told what *fois gras* actually is. Told instead which news headline to care most about and check they are right until tomorrow.

That house is a gloss powder puff. The near rolling lawns Halloween apple bushels nicey nice. The side where the Christmas bows will go. Careful of that, it's hot to the touch.

That house is a neglected Hammond organ. Look up close, the keys are all covered with spud dust and jewelry mew atop the black lacquer. What's inside the box. A lot of candles that don't get used because there's nothing to light the cigars with in that peach melba doll house built to scale.

The table legs were uneven without a matchbook. It was the newest piece of furniture in the house. The chairs too, of tan vinyl. I never leaned back though. They said things like singing is stupid. Sometimes I listened to their records that screamed. There were fourteen half-assed plastered-over holes above one of their heads. I am the archeologist of the last tenants. No one covered them with pictures. I thought of pasting supermarket stickers over them. Half-price sale. Use before expiry date. Special.

I was usually the only one who had to be there in the morning. The radio bleated out the Monday minus forty no surprise like weak bouillon soup.

At supper I swallowed and mentioned the well done spelling test. Pride never felt right seared by the watery beef and mealy turnip. The conspiracy theories and the gritty cynicism.

Poverty grieves for when I delighted guiltily in super new running shoes and sticker books. I was already wondering how I'd ever make a good living and give each of them a home where the paint was not made of mold. No smoke on the mirrors. I wanted to push seashells to their ears, thrust pussy willows to their fingers, but they were not soldiers who abandoned their orders when the eyes of their enemy opened theirs wide. I wondered about the TV places. Volcanos left black sand and how it would feel. Would the love of it cause my skin to grow over where it constantly sheds. Salamander sick with psoriasis. Or would it be as fragrant and blissfully tactile as I imagined.

So I just waited for the suppertime when on the chair my feet touched the ground and not mind the food touching on the plate. When I set down a copper carafe of wine reached for by all at the same time. Light laughter at that and lingered over good chocolate. And everyone was fine.

Understudy bird ready even through myopia and though the feathers are fitted for the others it was a life to yield in my Easter pink bones. Hollyhocks resistant stems indignant to the hurricane of that ordinary life.

Arms upside hands flat. Tough way to be held spinning giddy. A fleeting image of licking the pancake syrup plate clean. Looked straight into the candle stretching the flame. Early discovered talents cornered me, resigned to the love of eyes on me and settled for daily rebuke to remain on the edge of the crystal path.

Some music is difficult to count to but repetition engraves the heart with a flippant wave. The off-centre home stairs, the scratchy polyester sweaters, and science in its final stubbornness.

Dance through the implausible faint not from hunger or fatigue but the so much given up to rise too early for a Saturday and resin the soles so they stick me to the floor lest I begin to dream for desire for anything other than this standing for hours still arranged and rearranged until someone calls me to move.

I was hoping it was not so obvious through my poker face that I was thinking of things I'd like to have, I'd like to do. This might have been guessed at but I tucked my feet beneath my chair and kept counting cards anyway. This passive thoughtlessness carefully replaced by theory or debate, the debate loud and out of control, the moderator hired only because he had experience as a bingo caller but still these theories remained. Hypothesis the only way. To figure out the moment you were born would be to don a blindfold, turn around three times, flip through an old calendar and point to a random day. Of course even this would not have provided all the details I required to go further into my strange new science. But valuing mystery too I knew not many could ever visit the Galapagos Islands or drink from the water fountain on one of Saturn's moons. Perhaps it would be discovered as well how impatient I was, my teeth ground down Zamboni smooth while I waited for another hand to be dealt and perched atop a couple of phone books so as to be able to see above my mountain of chips.

That first time I was four you were much older
vowed to one day take over. It was my birthday
but it was only your age that ever mattered. I
ignored them, you hated them. Don't get me
wrong, I was glad you were there the day the guy
on the bus came up to us and you snarled. I
wonder what they're doing. Wait and see.
Meanwhile I have words for a fairweather friend.
As luck would have it. You were the one who with
a deep kiss pushed over the balcony into the
snowbank sweetest sixteen drunk and drama. You
made me silly with pride black hair dyed my
mother cried. It was easier to be like you than to
let you rule me.

This is Poly Sci. Head girl had a cold. She coughed into the sink. Her others dipped fingers in it and germed up their tongues. Tomorrow's going to be rhinitis under blankets so they can watch that stellar *Young and the Restless* that's going to be on.

Layla sat behind me in math. She tried to get me to talk to her so I would get a tick beside my name. My math mark was bad enough already. The teacher did it that way cause he was too shy to tell the kids to shut up.

Sean spat on me in the hallway. I didn't catch the cold. Don't get to stay home. Sean's dog story was praised. Mr. T held it above his head. I handed in my journal. *I don't think such a talented lad would spit on anybody.* In red.

StayInSchoolFool. The guidance counselor tried to train me in assertiveness. Showed me a 90 pound weakling at the back of an Archie comic. He was caught in a cool cat sandstorm. You've seen it before. It's been around since way before skinniness worked for Bill Gates. But I was not good at math like I guess he was. Charles Atlas drank eggs. I couldn't bring myself to do that so I must not really have wanted to change.

Make wait. I slaved over my yearbook quote. Got

to be one from that movie *Heathers*. Not too creative. The editor printed that I said let's rock grade ten with the initials of people who were not my friends.

I got contact lenses and somebody was looking at me twice. But I was still wearing the wrong brand of runners. Feet sopping from the grey slush. Damp was a pretty sympathetic companion.

This is Poly Sci. The girls didn't pretend not to be looking and enjoying it. I handed in my English journal, my judgments in Latin. *A lot of them have bad problems too.* In red at the bottom. If I had had fingernails I would have driven them into my palm.

I rode buses around all day and called the phone booth at the zoo that was built around a prairie dog colony years ago. No one ever picked up. I coloured the maps as assigned.

Spring was no break with malls teeming with clotted mouth girls. They called it puppy love. They didn't know how one day they'd be eating Paxil cookies feeling uncertain and guilty. And Sean will be the Pharma Rep. Pill samples in a box with a flower woman cartoon. The dog-eared dog story folded up in his wallet. *Dogs are people too*, at the bottom. Written in red.

To forget about the stuffed tweed rocking chair, the oval orange braid rug, the blue mountain pottery in the ersatz walnut wall unit, blue mountain swan, two blue mountain owls, owl and owlet. Where is this blue mountain anyhow. To forget about it and my allergic rhinitis eyes staring out from my grade one class picture, the only baby picture. Milky skin blotch pink. Because we had to wait too long in line at Sears. The plastic wood-grained particle board TV trays I ate from waiting for *Family Feud* to be over, waiting for the family feud to be over. To forget about it I was inspecting the African violets for mites. Because my eyes are best and I'm sorry cause I can't seem to make anything better. The cushion I turned over to hide the melt burn from the hot toffee pot I set down that time when the phone rang. To forget about it I was sloshing back whiskey sours. Later I would ruin the fuzzy teal bath mat and I'd not be permitted to forget about it.

Layla and I had been eating a lot of bananas. Not for the potassium or anything like that but so she could hang the peels up on her door and dry them out. Because they called it mellow yellow. We didn't laugh about anything any different. We guessed we did it wrong or something. But it was okay. Laughing at those same things made time stand back a while and let us be.

Layla's apartment was way nicer than at home where I still lived. I was glad she moved to the West End where I was. It was run down and dangerous but the gangs made for lively Sunday nights running home. Layla's parents gave her a personal alarm. We tried it out one day in the back alley. It sounded like a fweeping guinea pig sitting on a K-Mart clock radio.

Layla's roommate, who called himself Wheel although his real name was Stuart, was an animal whose strange habits we pored over. He gave us a blank look when we told him he was one letter short of being a Degrassi character. We called him Wheels anyway, but he was a little deaf in one ear so it couldn't bug him. He bought white sports socks and dyed them an enviro-conscious beige in a huge soup pot on the stove. He made millet loaves and we thought he was trying to levitate in his room with all the chimes and singing.

Layla worked at a fudge stand in Eaton Place and had to remember to wash her sticky apron every night. When she'd forget she'd furiously rub out the spots in the morning with Halsa shampoo for red highlights. It actually worked pretty well. I didn't find a job. I stayed up all night and slept until five. It was winter so I rarely saw daylight. Layla was concerned and asked her old favourite highschool teacher her opinion of the situation. Her teacher said it sounded like I was an alcoholic. The thing was I didn't drink those nights awake. I listened to a Las Vegas radio show about unexplained phenomena and conspiracy theories and laughed my head off. I wasn't even unhappy and I was surprised at Layla. She knew I only drank as much vodka as she did and the rest of them at the Macaroni Bar on the weekends. I was legal but still forced to show ID because they said I looked really young even with the worry groove across my forehead. Layla looked her age though. She told hilarious anecdotes to the table, mostly about fudge customers. I thought she could be an amazing writer but no one would know. Even though she wrote lengthy journal entries every night before bed, she tore them up the next day and burned them in a bowl of water. Wheels told her that wasn't a good thing to do.

I finally got the job but didn't show up on account of sleeping in all the time. When Layla took over the job I was happy about it. Layla was beginning to throw not-quite-done fudge at businessmen. So she became a prop girl at an improv theatre place and fell for the lighting guy. I thought he wasn't smart enough for her and that her enthusiasm would distance her from me. It was good to see her living contentedly though. In osmosis it felt like the way I still desired the stage, not to be behind it but on it. When it ended it was like walking away from that one thing that made me feel real. In fact both Layla and I had always been on one stage or another in tap shoes or little league jazz bands. The only one we either wouldn't accept or weren't ready for was that one in Shakespeare, it being all the world.

We were getting older and wondered if we were supposed to stop liking to chew super sour gum and drink Slurpees at the same time. Layla entrusted her name with her fate. She felt she had no choice to be either a meter reader or a receptionist at a talent agency specializing in biker types. I should've been thinking about what to do also, but I only leafed through women's magazines incredulous at $650 beaded clutches next to articles about eating disorders, fad diets and champion female rowers. I didn't even let anyone know my opinions.

I missed Layla even before I decided to leave the dull brown city. I knew our first series of letters would quickly fizzle out when we both had little to say and I floated from apartment to apartment every July 1st forgetting to send her my new address. When I would turn twenty-one, twenty-five, then thirty I would shake my head in disbelief that Layla would be growing older too. Always having been more responsible than me, she'd be well set up in the world we had always tried to ignore. She would dye her hair back to a respectable colour, accept her parent's old Saab, and obsessively re-edit her university papers long after the classes had ended and she'd passed them with flying colours. Maybe she'd start going by her middle name, Elizabeth, and take a job as an arts administrator, and I would never have to worry about her the way she had always worried about me.

There was another notion, which I preferred. That she was traveling to every corner of the world, but stage or not she wouldn't be acting at all, she'd be dancing without choreography. I smiled for real at the thought.

And we would be sad and lucky remembering the notebook we filled with practical joke ideas we never actually went through with, or the film we tried to make with a video camera which ended up having serious continuity issues due to all those ever changing hair colours. We would feel our old warmth but have trouble with the details of all the stuff we did, especially the night of the banana peels, and whatever Wheels had been chanting in the next room.

It might have all come back to us if we had seen cans of Mellow Yellow soda pop in the store. But it wouldn't because you can't seem to find it anywhere anymore. They might have stopped making it altogether.

Spring city run off, frayed-handled bag by the door at the ready, but for what. I take while I remain. Walls stay half-way painted. There is an art to inflating the list price of imagination.

Being in university felt like bad theatre. Somehow I'd been given a loan for one semester, but hadn't paid tuition yet, hadn't bought a single book. However, I had given a friend five hundred dollars for her unpaid credit card bills. And then of course ever early into late night was two for one rum and Coke specials. It was adding up.

The only school I had been able to get into was the one that looked like a mall. The halls were not hallowed but green glass and dirty metal. I was considered a mature student. A crook came to my mouth whenever I considered that. But I had it better than when I was in highschool six years before, when I skipped most classes but music, and charmed even the math teacher into passing me because of my talents in that realm. I guess I was supposed to be there, packed like another drone sardine, but not smiling so banally on the escalator, trying to remember where room A3271 was.

A little man with perpetual spittle on his wiry beard mentioned at least four times every class how he was a renowned expert on Shakespeare, and then went on to talk about paradigms in *Beowulf*. I could never hear him because I was trying so hard to keep my eyes open. All I really had energy for was plopping lime wedges into my rum and Cokes, writing letters all night that would remain unsent, and thinking about moving the programmable coffee maker next to the bed so I could just reach across to refill my cup all morning. Days without eating much. I couldn't remember the last time I had a good appetite. I tried to force myself to eat, but it always came back up later, along with the acrid coffee, a total waste of two or three or five dollars.

When the time came for the *Beowulf* exam I responded to question two furiously, but had no memory of what I'd written until I got it back, obviously the lowest grade in the class, as it was on the very bottom of the pile. It was apparently so terrible the Shakespeare man held it up as an example of nonsense. I supposed everyone guessed it was my paper because as I was leaving the class he mouthed, "Come see me."

But I never enjoyed people being so enthralled with my flaws, especially when they were pointed out to me with a quizzical, "But you are so obviously an intelligent young woman." I decided to trick myself into believing I'd simply forgotten about my other exam in the other English course. I realized I had to do something. The loan would soon run out, the bank would want its money back once it learned I wouldn't be continuing with school.

On top of the television lay my violin in its beat up case, and I could just about hear it sigh oh what are we going to do with you. I hadn't played it in months. Mara, an acquaintance, had pointed this out, as well as a myriad of my other failings, at some party when we were the only two people left in the kitchen besides a hippy who lay snoring under the kitchen table.

"I don't understand why you don't play anymore. I used to love to go to your shows. And whenever I see you you have a drink and a cigarette in your hand. Are you like okay?" I didn't have the time to tell this person I hardly knew that I saw her regularly with a vodka tonic, or sitting in the school newspaper room obviously not going to her Women's Studies classes, because she went on, "And you know, I took Psych last semester and I think maybe——" So there I was in the middle of an impromptu one-man intervention, actually wondering if when I turned around I'd find there was no longer a door out of the room.

I would've laughed, but I was afraid I might be sick. I was seeing stars. This Mara went on like the hour and a half long *Beowulf* paradigms. Mara said finally, "Yes. You are wasting your talent and these good years." At that moment I didn't want to touch the violin ever again. It was like hearing some crooning daycare worker encourage your finger painting because for once you didn't just sit staring at the piece of paper. And then feeling indignant ever after, not painting at all because you just wanted to be left alone, clicking the coloured counting beads back and forth.

But some good could come out of this. I could sell the violin. Take the last of the loan money and hop a bus somewhere where no one's preconceived notions of my potential are not yet dashed.

Mara called me a couple of times, finding my number she'd said, by dialing 411 and she hoped I didn't mind. She wanted to go for coffee but I told her I was busy with internship applications, or another time that I was working on an embroidered wall hanging for a gallery show. If nothing else I had a quick reserve of imagination.

I stared at the violin case, perfectly ready to not be surprised if the thing spoke to me in the accusing voice of a brash New York city cab driver from under the black and duct tape. I snapped the case open and lifted out the violin and bow. Placing it under my chin, I half shrugged, but as I began to hear Bach's concerto for two violins in D minor in my head, my apathy began to dissipate. Yet both the fact that I might enjoy playing again and the fear that my fingers wouldn't remember what to do made me feel a little ill. But I had a secret left.

Whenever I got a cold, or suffered such intense nausea I could not eat, or lay in the dark with one of those raging migraines, I actually hoped, pleaded with nebulous deities that I had something, not serious, but which would lay me up for months in the hospital. Something fate had thrown my way which would allow me to lie in bed and let others focus on how to give me some kind of future. The quiet sympathy of nurses who would change my IV and the silent accolades of those administering painful tests which I would not wince from or complain about. I would be a model patient. My virtues would be obvious to the doctors and nurses and orderlies and patients. I would take the time to thank the lady who came in to empty the trash cans, and the man with the floor polisher. I would be seen by all as one of courage, curiosity, empathy, sweetness. I didn't go so far in my imagination as being terminal, just chronic. I knew those who truly are sick are the stoic ones, and that the meaning they find in their afflictions is not in being ill itself, but in their reasons for fighting: their families, getting out of the sterility and gloom of the hospital to work in their gardens, to stuff themselves with rich food, to sit with friends and drink wine and listen to music. I wasn't deriving any peace or contentment out of these simple joys of life lately. In truth, all I was doing was sticking out my bottom lip, holding my breath, shaking my head, and being perfectly willing to go stand in the corner. None would allow me my time to pout and no one would cajole me out of it with a bowl of mint chocolate chip ice cream. And there is no time to pout when you have to pay rent, make small talk with acquaintances, separate paper from plastic for the recycling.

I played a single note on the violin. The sound must have startled the room, which had been utterly silent and still for such a long time. I put the violin back into its case, then cut a large piece out of a velvet dress I no longer wore. I went down to the local Metro station with my violin and bag, and set up the piece of velvet at my feet near the escalator. I took out the violin, and started playing the Bach concerto, but instead of playing the sad *adagio* I started to play the *allegro* movement. Of course it was only one violin not two, but it still sounded like something. It was rush hour, and people looked dejected and pasty. I noticed people at the top of the escalator look around to see where the music was coming from, and then pointedly look away, some feigning confusion over which direction they were going. The heat and the sound of the trains and the huge screen advertisements were beginning to make me feel it was a waste of time, when an old man with a small boy in a stroller stopped to listen. The man nodded and smiled, and the boy clapped his hands. The man leaned over and said to the boy joyfully, "Musica Musica!" and "Mooska! Mooska!" the child repeated. The man took the boy out of the stroller and gave him a dollar coin, and they both approached me. The boy dropped the dollar in my case, and I stopped playing for a moment because it looked like the man was going to say something.

"Thank you so much," I said.

"No no no. Thank you to you my dear. I played the violin since I was no bigger than my grandson. I brought my violin all the way to Canada with me. But now the old hands shake too much, and the arthritis. But your Bach is so lovely. You must be very busy but you know, I wished to find somebody to teach my grandson when he gets older. I will give you my telephone number. You can think it over okay?"

"Oh. Well, yeah I actually think I would like to do that yes. Thank you."

"Wonderful! You look like a very nice girl. And so talented. Call me up then and we will arrange it. Of course we must wait until his hands are a little bigger but he grows so fast! We must be getting on our way now but we will be very glad to hear from you soon. Say bye to the nice girl Anthony."

"Bye bye!"

I smiled and waved to them as they melted into the crowd. I looked at my hands, stretched my fingers. It'd be fun to teach a little kid to play.

I looked at the huge clock by the Metro track. It was nearing five. I put the violin back in the case and set out for home. I was getting hungry.

I consider just cutting them all off. This means no more waiting and wondering. This is how that Carpenters song "Solitaire" becomes the pitifully humorous number one tune on the soundtrack to my life. I wouldn't wish it on anyone but perhaps everybody is being held hostage by doubt. Tapping fingers chewing the nails tossing and turning lying still willing the ceiling to spell out the right answers. Cleaning the whole house with smiling intentions bigger mess than when we started. The alignment of planets might be causing all this. But unfortunately the world's one celestial chiropractor had a year long waiting list and a really snotty secretary. Blame is futile. Or else blame futility itself. Campaign to have it taken out of the dictionary. Even after everything the world might have been too soft on me. I could just give in to that bleach smelling impulsivity. Shoplift, bang up my wrists and knees violet blue. Try and pass myself off as an angry old lady from Beaconsfield who writes letters to the editor every day which always get printed. To look in the mirror and see only myself at that hour of the present unleashes freedom. Flood free to leave by the front door. Good thing not to have to look at that old hallway lined with the photos I had asked and asked to be taken down and they won't and I don't know quite why anybody else would want to remember. Does everyone feel this way. When the voicemail lady says the box is full I figure maybe they are weary of sitting around comparing notes. The odd thing is all the horoscopes start advising the same things for every sign and though I've been pining for anyone anything to tell me what to do I put it off until tomorrow and the solitaire passes the time.

Your quilt is not yet finished so why not stay until it is heavy enough to keep you warm. You cannot stand it when your pictures and paintings never hang straight so you take them all down and stow them away. The spaces they leave are white, untouched by your tobacco paint. Your plants are all made of silk and you never did get another cat. Your quiet heart quiet mind off of a quiet tongue. Maybe some envy how you can go without speaking for a day or three without having made any vow with a gong, without a thrush throat, without resentment, without a doubt. With something lovely of thought. Lovely enough to wait for.

Never needed angel craft. Hover lone block. Walking fast to get back to the wonder of being lost in this old and weeping city when it was new and vast. Did not hide in layered sloth silk or murder sleep with hesitation pills. Time didn't know there would ever be a time when scars would be quite some gift. Sand stuck in these days and that narrowest place in the hourglass will quicken. Steps to running turning back round so as not to be against the tunneling embittered wind.

Fuzz daze caffeine over tired clever PIN number still looking over my shoulder. Theme birthday parties knights of the round table paper Barbie table cloth and noise horns. Like a mouthful of loose change. Oddly enough the new coins have the worst taste. The folks with three watches on each wrist four walls clock calendar clock calendar clock one finger stop the pendulum and try again and make up for it. Can't concentrate can't concentrate cubicle wars and errand plod. Satellite TV channel choices coming close to outnumbering cold remedies and lip repair. Want to revisit youth's haunts. Ill at ease not to belong there. The songs which used to rake through my nerves like the little tool for rock gardens now grate them so there is what looks like a frustrated flower bed but is only waiting for joyful rain. There's a way away from the syndromes of sick buildings and surly security guards. Quiet space not a thing to evade or amend. Time enough to spring step or cross-legged forgiving slouch. A meditation. Not so much is spoiled or delivered to the ungrateful. So I am bored. Cast as a sidewinder fossilized in desperate need. Can slow my pulse simply by seeing the sound on the graph. Crush worry in my palm as over autumn leaves.

I cut the crusts off the weeds below my window. My bite has always been uneven and silver braces never chose which way. Some sustenance to stain the hollow's protestations. The little park is a nice place to lay and make believe you're about to go wading in the fountain.

I lack initiative. I'm not a leader. The counselor guides with a sailboat letter opener. The application has been denied.

It's just those blues to make a note of that which the boys make a joke of. I push my bed to face North *feng shui* to shuck off bad luck. I spend a little more on serenity incense, consider whether it might actually be working. I sit on the side of the bus which won't show through the window the Zellers where I tried to work for two weeks. I couldn't stand to hear my own voice over the loudspeaker. And there was always a clean up on aisle seven where the kids got too excited over the talking trikes or in the ladies shoe aisle where housewives got upset when they realized the leather was vinyl.

I go out for menthol 100s, make a day of it, idle chit chat with twenty strangers. Headaches aren't so bad with a reason and I'm trying to give up on alt-health web searches and the endless information.

Please send your poems in the body of an e-mail. Payment is exposure.

Feels better to window shop incensed and incredulous at the sight of five hundred dollar *papier mâché* lamps and little twenty dollar boysenberry jams.

Are you a natural helping person? Are you a people pleaser? Can you say no? Are you a bossanova kinda girl?

I mistake night for morning and drop a Masters thesis into the bathtub by accident. The proofread red bleeds and the paper swells. I wonder if I should get an illuminated applause sign for my place.

I do not have to photocopy my CV for the privilege of doing the Wal-Mart cheer and being forced to write cheques printed on musical note paper. My body does not have to end Elastoplast brittle and sun damaged to tell my story. I do not have to hope for the freedom of levitation. I can forgive, my sin was out of spite. I can dance without having had to drink. I can smile at the crabby man driving the bus. I can dust my eyes a tacky eighties teal green.

I'm all over the break. Touch trees torch journals

laze in the tundra. Rebel against the organic tea package which says to steep for five minutes. I wait only about a minute. I know it's perfectly fine that way.

Our women weathered in sanguine murk but here in eggshell white light reflecting no more of the only stale bread sick love no more. You slice watermelon pieces mouth sized. Secret corner smile as to how you came across it so late in the season. You curl in quilt and rocking chair as the baby sleeps at last. No proverbial home and country motif undermining this space. Their own voices grace the walls. Core out of the core. Bruisings and badly set bones above the mantle, on the mantle all their sorrowed and smiling eyes. No one observes or takes notes, no cold interviews by whomever is Tuesday's smirk judge with one loaded question phrased a thousand ways. Because they did get out. From here they go back into theirs. Walking through life in all walks of life looking out on the big backyard nature as yet so sheltered and at rest their deserved November promise is warm alive come spring time.

Somebody's whispering she didn't eat today. Sits down. Says are you okay, why not come on with me. That's not my problem, I say. But the guy doesn't believe it's romantic saving me to feed me steak and eggs. My manager wouldn't complain about the height of my hem or finding the half truths on my resume. Someone thinks my name should be Light or Summer Rain, frowning when they learn it is so plain. Little passion it would be for them to force their voices lower to utter it at three in the morning on top of cheap cotton sheets. I don't complain to anyone about my dizzy spells. I'm supposed to be a half health junkie almost inhaling a carrot mistaking the hand which is holding the cigarette. Someone's pointing out dark circles under my eyes, very chapped lips, the fact that I write with an ordinary bic in that book. Someone's looking over my shoulder, it is only a grocery list, always someone to disappoint. Shock like a weather vane whether vain or not boxed up accomplishments. Some idea I thought might never have been thought of. I shouldn't have turned on the television story at eleven. There's a flower, looks nice, surprise no scent. But beauty is a liar. Velvet will give you an unpleasant spine shiver when you rub it the wrong way. No one whispers I wonder what she has to say.

Quick kitten with the fly and he would even find a way to jump from desk to top of shelf to get at it so he does but loses sight of its black ribbon wings as ball of wool at Woman's feet intrigues. The clicking of her knitting needles not unlike the finger tapping of Man trying to figure out the last crossword clue while their voices begin to duel with those of the neighbour's children practicing lay ups in the laneway using a hoop which will offer no challenge come summer's end. You can hear their bones creaking through the nights with every window open. But where is that fly now and if he could catch it would it vibrate like that other striped kind. Would it leave his mouth swollen and cause Woman to scold and croon and Man to chortle and rise to take the dog out. There is the fly between window and screen slamming facet eyes again and again for that tiny hole to open air. He will jump down and get it before it can ride to the honeysuckle on avarice garbage. Before Woman and Man come to the end of their every third Sunday re-hashing of a thirty some odd years ago wedding that had almost never been.

Slander you truth. Just making her work for the 38 cent tip so bravado dolled. Send down on you alone a boil plague but you would only nod and nod shiny lick your lips ecstatic eyes yes rolling back in status elepticus. Then you would come around to agreeably suck on your own fester pus lesions sprawled naked upon your Oma's star-burst pattern quilt. Tales told second hand dull and then dull. Anyone would rather stare at the paint drying web cam. Lessons from an ordained blob of dough. Trying to flatten us all down cheap hiking boot in the trash can. Little guilt of an image of the one you neglected to mention coming at you clawing your boozed red rosacea head. She's success and so is she. Any lady'd rather Elmer Fudd than you. Suck dolt drooler. Leave my girl alone.

Why do I bother when the banks are bursting at the seams. I hold my hand up to anything that is fluid, anything that can restore itself. My cuticles are ripped up and there's that strange spot on my shoulder that I should really get checked out.

Red fern spreading out under Dog Star. Manufactured nature no match for the perfect chaos and the fossils giddy they'll not be put out on display. This cell no prison and time is not frozen even while I helplessly attempt to solder it out. Not my only enjoyment when I am not giving answer with a cough. I am owning up to those chin stroking perusals. To keep everything in some barbed pen would be to lose all my rush after and then where would I be.

Red fern sunny farm overgrown Pachabele Canon circles quiet vultures and the mood here's not grim. And I'll never make it so real. True beauty won't stick to those white adhesive labels.

I secretly want something to compare myself to. Do so. Test tube and the lab planet are just as polluted. I arrange the meeting with one hand bandaged, scraped knuckles of the other, when I see how the water rock air have renewed themselves quicker than my own skin.

Duchess with wan smile. My tea brewed an hour
kept hot until I muse to take a sip. If this one is not
my Duke I will know in the way his brow is set. My
lamps are lit long into the night. I sleep. Roses are
tossed. Have I ever been seen with straight wet
hair. My shoulders and face dust arsenic white.
Each new morning is a Renaissance to my pride.
The crowds below watch me not touch my cake.

On the train a tax attorney considers his cheerful new receptionist Layla and the notebook she scribbles in while eating her lunch at her desk. And how this morning his stealthy eye happened to glance over what he'd been curious about since she'd been hired. Her loops seemed to describe eastern autumn trees and he shifted his weight and gulped a little having thought it might be a monthly budget. She had said something about maybe having to find a cheaper place.

He picks out a notebook for himself after five. He doesn't realize he could get twelve for the price of this one at Dollarama. The cover is sturdy deep maroon, a place to place his name and his pen's a fountain with his title and e-mail on the side and his address he sort of wishes could be something unusual but that would not be acceptable.

Just how does Layla do it. He tries to rhyme. Says to himself he's been relying on spell check for too long a time.

And just what about the elm on his lawn he never saw progress though he had it planted by men whose arms made him shy with his wife because he knew she noticed theirs. As she sighed over the soapy sink the brand new dishwasher is on the fritz again.

About his squash games with clients having been seen in the eighties on film. That is what an exec does to charm them in the afternoons. And then not to let on he loathes the taste of scotch and that new throbbing beat they've put behind the old jazz that was just fine the way it was.

They write a lot about childhood don't they. Mussy haired doubting with dep coffee and ash-trays. A picture in their chests. He's wondered about them when he takes a risk on a new café. His childhood no consequence and most of them hardly out of theirs but maybe they remember bare feet in mud pies and how the afternoon making them went by in a flash and at night how they slept feeling loved and safe.

If only he could've taken a picture of her open page with his cellphone and understand how to begin.

Flower that ocean there schoolboy. Fishing trip with grandfather. The way he proposed which no one knows but her. Sedate golf course watching his drive sail or better still the one home run he hit surprised everyone because he was just a math geek. Cognac in the study with Mozart, the lake cottage where that really might have been a flying saucer, hard won success. Weekend flannel shirts puttering in the garage. None of this is right.

Once I have a chance to choose what colour suits me I'll have to empty my closets. I'll have to prevent sportscasts. I can't tell whether what's beside the old moon is another star or a satellite or a planet. What are you listening to.

I've been getting a lot of calls lately with no one there. The ones in the afternoon make me more nervous than the ones at two AM and star 69 tells me nothing except that the service costs fifty cents. I close my eyes and imagine that the horns of the Mac trucks outside are really those of steamships. Because I'd live right by the sea to rush up and taste it.

I look everywhere for lined grey paper because bleach is bleaching the streets and our arteries. If I find it I can't afford it. It is way cheaper to do the wrong thing. I am always so thirsty now. Is it some kind of low sugar or am I dreaming. I pick up a copy of *Cosmo* with college girls telling how they get extensive plastic surgery in preparation for Florida spring break and I wonder if I am missing something.

I try vanilla fabric softener. Smells like cookies. The world is in a gilt frame full clouds blind bats trees twist and rivers are stitched up with reeds. I am the treble clef not tied to the coda. Infrequent

rainbows stretch on my elation. And the world's
not plastic.

Mid-morning winter long shadows neighbours come and go. Mid-morning strange hours front door. Are there shady dealings. Employment centre yellow teeth from behind the bullet proof vent to talk through can't hear me. Just imagine walking a mile to flip filet-o-fish. Normal's off shooting arrows everywhere and the only good doctors are the ones who admit they're not quite sure and then go find out. The barometric pressure migraines, the TV dots, force the eyes long past a decent bedtime. The pocket lint which won't buy me any time. Six AM means donning the minimum wage smock and waiting for the walkie-talkie order of which aisle to set up the flashing blue light. Laundry soap double coupon econo size Mr. Freeze. There's a long haul trucker diesel romance list of CB radio handles written on cashier tape. To haul tomatoes, on the outside imperfections that hide their cool colourful taste. To fly out of the city with simple diner coffee in those white cups with waitresses named Rita or Ginny who'll talk about the hard luck but only when asked and everyone laughing at the wonderfully bad jokes the counter men make. The road with its trusting fading yellow lines the scratchy AM country radio and every coming golden purple sunrise.

Grass has shed itself upon a rote blade. Some floss. Hairline fracture of the femur and then the miss. That loose step at the bottom. Made it up to the top of the hill that is so embarrassed of having grown over garbage.

Salty taste always on my tongue. The all consuming consume it brick by brick up the bridesmaid at my cousin's second wedding. Reception buffet marzipan swan. I pocket shrimp cocktail. I can because I've changed out of the red velvet gold trim Christmas time dress into my favourite tattered jeans, favourite soft blue sweater, less loved sneakers, they're too new yet. To my cousin's chagrin. The least expensive caterer plastic cups of canned cherry pie filling black forest in place or in lieu of an eighteen tier wedding cake. There are no penguin waiters here, you have to lean over or push through the line to get some.

The wedding and the two week holiday respite from all the deciding, and the deciding can be pushed back, is pushed back, and of course empty. And I'll think a while under those pin stars when I feel faint. Maybe the deciding can wait a while longer. There's no time to think on it now anyway not with the groom leaning on a chair telling me a story of how he once went out with a chick and when he met her roommate it was weird cause he liked her better cause she was way hotter. He waits for me to ask him, well what did you do, but I don't and he makes his way over to the open bar for a fuzzy navel.

I'm hungry and every table an aunt or a church lady chews on boiled roast beef and I hate the sight as much as standing next to some guy on a crowded bus whose fingers keep bringing up orange taco chips to his greasy mouth. All this extra food will spoil. No one will think of where to donate it. But I load my plate and go into the cloak room where I find a secret spot between two fur coats which couldn't belong to any of my cousin's wedding guests. Do not taste just touch, churn it smooth like an industrial ice cream mixer. Remember the elementary school trip to the candy factory and the chocolate peanuts coming out shiny wet. Sort of sad they couldn't stay that way. And the large man flipping thick lengths of peppermint around his arms. Still shiny too, still glistening metallic pink to harden and turn matte.

The plastic plate does not hold enough but I can't go back inside and have everyone cheer me on to twist again with my cousin like I never did last summer. I wouldn't be able to fight the urge to straighten the groom's clip-on bow tie, to give my cousin a little dignity since everyone has a feeling this is the last chance for happiness.

It's when I hear the Ukrainian songs that I know no one will come looking for me. They're too busy spinning around and around not knowing or caring. I go to the table again and load up three plates this time, balancing them perfectly. The responsible part of my head notes if things don't work out next semester I would probably make a good waitress.

I never wear a watch so I won't know how long it takes to eat. Which seems strange it always being like a contest. I taste nothing or everything. The salt is sweet cream. The airy vinegar, solid dull chewy white bread, the black forest, grade one Elmer's thick paste.

The only one who would ever know is my other cousin Ellen, the first to almost graduate BSC. Who gave it up for Glasgow and reading about science on her own time and stopped feeling bad about not coming to the family's weddings years ago. If Ellen were here she wouldn't say much about what she was doing now but tell me to be the waitress of the year and leave.

And it seems more right as I look at my blotchy face in the mirror. My eyes are bloodshot from the power of the force of release. It seems right because there's no either or. It cannot go on. There's no destiny for spaghetti sauce splattered cumberbunds, nor for shaky hand spittle mouth profs wheezing *Beowulf* for six weeks. Cold porcelain wakes you up this way.

I carry trays of food half-decent. I'll have to turn my head while they eat it and then it won't be so bad. And calender *X* days until my flight when I'll savour one or two fresh mangoes on the beach and just enjoy them.

What causes you to lose your speech from behind thick bars of the shark cage. So much life all one organism. You are thought full mouth when you are awake. Fearful icicles on eyelashes your brow set low and hard you're tired but you smile, glide across the room, take note of who has the camera, and turn the other way. Plankton pop off ideas and the rest of the matter too. But not until the lack is seen at the top. Listen, someone knows just how you feel. A light on late at night across the way, the television crying not to be switched. Dare to start a new book, try to paint or sew or sing along with Sinatra. You've got no porch swing. Never curled up but rocking in that cage four sides up down across. Once in a while somebody knocks. Which way is the knob familiar with the walls. They feel something like clay all of a sudden before hardened by the sun. The picture you painted in there once a cityscape since some country starred sky too ornate to touch. Scuffed over that postmodern tone canvas on the floor, flat done when you could not make up words. Taste like nickel on your tongue. You were so certain that if you did try to form what you were thinking that the idea might toil itself out as something like brittle Germanic or all rolling rs and then what would anyone think. Just getting past their surprise at your trying to actually utter. But the sharks are mild, those teeth filed round. It has always been

only a graceful invitation. Simply say the words.
All right I will come along.

Descends. Slow and thick as syrup undiluted black with gash. Too many star patterns seen from the moon in sinking sand. Early morning hours no respite even a half hour Athena sleeping sound. Indelible. Sharp edged jewels. You have rubies four eyes. Starlings watch me watch the traffic from the dilapidated balcony. Every day an eclipse, the kind you can't look into. I do. It must be a myth that you never end up blind. And come in watch at the window, draw close the curtains quick. The hymns are ominous, the voices octaves above sound.

Noah's three by three includes me though the rain drives down in a state of only gentle mania but mania all the same. Maybe in the end there will be an end and for the rest of them some point to a particle of safety. Teach myself to learn the how to of this trust in the six meals a day warm balanced colours. Never mind about sending out the doves. There is no bleach light anymore to pollute the North Star. The compasses point away from that hollow South. Forward on to hearth warm. Where these waters have frozen depths our best guess. The breakers seamless now with nature's faith that we will leave it to fuse again. Now that, that would be rare.

True family, ones of the unblood, the true the chosen and yes she can, into her we seep. She drives the shrapnel further in with every word of silence. The rest of us chew down our nails wring our hands hold tight dolls. Stoplight stepladder spat spite. Was it her earthquake which rocked my cradle clear across the room. We think she comes from the East, red white and doom our ridiculous rhyme. I walk down the street with eyes closed anyway anyone of us will will the way. Tap the trap the dripping tap the wings the wands the rut. Who we are all breathing and then some.

My birthday is fast approaching. It is so cold I want to turn the heat on but I can't do that. Beg back insomnia not this night after night terror cross-eyed lamb. Out pouring salt on the theatre's portico I considered for a moment I wasn't and was one of the ones standing for ovation but no. Confusion is caloric. I am filling out. In my nice tidy quake I bit right through my tongue but did not feel a thing because heaven only knew where I was. They must be controlled. I can do that and blue Holly Golightly's mean reds away. But I have to think of what I have done and make a note that the plight of the river is to make it to the ocean in time. The telephone could ring when it is not. The tap in the kitchen might randomly turn itself on. Mother Goose retires for the night, her rhymes repeat themselves on and on. I count nickels and dimes. I can tell who is not in love. Sweet miracles in the lives of bees. White fluffy kittens sold toilet paper on TV and I bought it. My eyes fluttering under REM early this morning had a bird trapped and flying wild in my place and then received a ducky card it's your birthday so go quackers with a six hundred dollar cheque, my disgusting Hydro bill paid. I do love all of the colours and long for what I can't see and flee from my mind and little words written in dew and kind today perhaps today.

Layla refused to mistake this feeling for hunger. But that would mean defining it as something else, which she was unable to do at the moment. She opened a bag of black pepper and lime potato chips and plunged a handful into a container of sour cream. The other day she'd read an article about *eating mindfully*, but thought that an absurd thing to try to do with junk food. She actually hoped the MSG would somehow preserve the blasé within her. She refused to care about what Jack was doing right now. Besides, she'd already seen it once with her own eyes, in the four poster bed they'd bought together at an estate sale. She'd had to wash the sheets and pillow cases three times that night, to get the barmaid's candy perfume and the whatever else out. Her cat Theo had gotten literally pissed off at Jack as well. Cat pee and the rest of it seemed to smell a bit like the liquid penicillin she'd had to take as a child for her frequent ear infections.

Layla got lucky in that her dancer friend Tara was going away on tour. "You can sublet my place for four months, hun. And screw Jack. No, don't actually," she'd said.

Tara's place was made for things like eating mindfully. Mandala art covered the walls and books with titles like *Anxiety Free Through Tai Chi,* and *Your*

Inner Buddha lined the shelves. There was no evidence anywhere of Tara being a dancer. No Martha Graham biographies, no *Thinking Body / Dancing Mind*. Which were essentially all zenny too, but Layla supposed she didn't want such titles sticking out of her bookshelf. Layla suspected Tara wanted to erase her talent and go become a corporate lawyer, or at least a real estate agent. In spite of the zen surroundings, rock garden and all, Layla rejected the energy in the room, which was almost impossible to avoid.

Layla was glad she'd told none of her friends her new telephone number. Having to explain what had happened again and again reminded her of how tired she'd gotten after coming to school in grade three with a cast on her arm after 'trying to skate like a boy'. The endless, "Aw what happened?" and the stupid sentiments and cartoons scrawled on the plaster in purple marker were more attention than she could bear. She'd brought Theo with her though, and he sat silent and protective beside her on the red velvet couch. She would have to get up tomorrow and shower, and take the Metro to her job at the magazine, proofreading poetry all day that was supposed to be 'socially and politically conscious', but which was almost always some long winded spiel on the metaphor of the garbage dump. But who was she to judge. She had written poems like this herself in dollar store notebooks with surfers on the covers.

She often sent her grandfather this writing and could hear him sputter and see him toss it into his study's fireplace, all those miles away in New Brunswick. He respected her enough to be unforgiving. "This is crap Layla! Don't bother with the writing poetry my girl!"

Layla thought of her grandfather now, who was no doubt lying in front of the TV, most likely eating foods forbidden to him due to his gastrointestinal ailments which left him keeled over in the morning. He had been a professor of philosophy and had the right books on his mantle, but made no secret of the fact that he watched what his colleagues called trash. Nick and Jessica. *Extreme Makeover*.

"Ah, you are writing a paper, maybe on the sociological ramifications of the blahdididty blah blah?" a bearded and goggle-eyed fellow who was a fellow had asked him, dry sherry in hand.

"No, blast!" her grandfather had said. "Must I read Sartre and *Finnegan's Wake* every minute? These shows neither disgust me nor am I ashamed to turn them on. They simply cause my shoulders to settle below the tops of my ears for once. Better than any hot bath or ninety dollar an hour masseuse I can tell you."

He assumed Layla watched these shows too,

and she started doing so just to please him. Unlike him though she tried to keep this fact a secret. She would quickly shut the TV off whenever Jack came into the room. She'd open his Communications textbook and pretend she was totally absorbed in it. She resented that she had to hide her guilty pleasure, especially when her grandfather would call and ask her if she had seen *Big Brother* tonight? Caleb and Stephanie had been flirting shamelessly in the hot tub over mango smoothies no doubt spiked with rum! In a low voice she'd answer that she had, and that she was also starting to hate Carley, who had started 'borrowing' Becca's clothes, and was obviously trying to come between Rachel and Craig.

Now that she was alone she indulged in her chips and sour cream as she pictured her grandfather eating pastrami and onion sandwiches while they both watched hours of reality shows. When she'd told him about what had happened with Jack he'd harrumphed, "What do you expect sweetheart, that shock of red hair, and half of a degree in Communications of all things, filthy rich family. Never choose a partner who has an all consuming sense of entitlement."

She was thinking she'd go and visit her grandfather once her sublease ran out. It would be nice to sit in his study with the big screen TV. She'd make him his sandwiches, and follow up with scotch and soda, maybe try and cajole him into taking Maalox now and then. She should probably take it herself. Her stomach had been curdling and burning a lot lately.

She turned on Nick and Jessica and saw that Nick was exasperated with Jessica spending eight hundred dollars on a pair of sling back Versace shoes. At the end though they ate endangered swordfish and chocolate truffle soufflé while being serenaded by someone like Placido Domingo's son. They sipped champagne from the most delicate champagne flutes Layla had ever seen.

One day she glanced at a tabloid at the grocery store. *Nick and Jessica splitsville!!!* it blurted. Layla thought that was really too bad. She wondered if Jessica would get the champagne flutes in the settlement. She should call her grandfather since he would probably have good insight on the whole deal, or be so disillusioned he'd go back to his Sartre. Probably not. There were new shows starting in the fall. It seemed as if there was a never ending supply of reality.

Spread every blessing thick coat slow molasses lock the sweet with vinegar and paint from an old brush. Today is the last day to decide on the crime that will repay every debt. But then this turn of mind with the breakwater, this relief for new spring will give. Never taken for granted these purity days no commas to break evening between dunes penning apology and thank you notes for those scorned and generous. And the fleets are coming so welcoming.

The couches are all taken up and there's always one person who is too shy to sit close to the person beside and so spends the whole night with a spring in their back hoping the alcohol will render the discomfort unnoticeable. Everybody else sits on the dusty floor and wonders when the people who live here will get the cats a litter box or whether they actually enjoy the smell as a statement of some kind. People pretend to like or hate the band depending on the reactions of the others and consciously cover their glasses with their own fingerprints to deny there were other ones left there from the other night, wrong evidence. It is only the next day in the cold winter sunlight shining in the café, after so much coffee, that I feel like I might risk asking one or two of those who'd been there whether they too sensed some dark energy in that place. When they agree too enthusiastically, saying they always leave feeling weird or sick, I wonder why they are already talking about going back tonight and why I'll probably go too. And I do and I notice someone has brought over a plant lush and flowering and everyone knows that within days it will be withered and sorry yet nobody takes it home and places it on their window sill. Someone who is usually snide surprises with her ethereal voice but the music gets to be too much and so do the unnatural silences. There are those who forget themselves in the corners and I wonder what their sad laughter is all about. The tin can ashtrays overflow and the songs all start to sound the same with no discernable downbeat. But when the choir comes on and cools down the room most start stepping out of the jet stream and later leave for the mountain, not brave enough to sit together in a circle but alone or in twos or threes. They exchange jewelry, tell bad jokes with wonderfully graceless gestures, and enjoy the perfect and strange ten degree February weather so much more pleasant than that overheated stuffy winter room.

I buy *Spin* magazine, that periodical which I used to read religiously at fifteen. Green lights next to the music reviews tell me which bands to go right out and get. Good rabbit. Little pot of tea. Greaseman at the table across. I lift the magazine to hide the face he's already seen.

Can I take your photo. Polaroid instamatic looks just like the one that was stolen. Showed up in the pawn shop down the street but no serial number or defining scratches, no way to retrieve. Can I take your photo. You'd be so good with less make up and smiles you know. I've worked with those girls with the emotional difficulties. Snaps the photo and shakes it dry. I want to but do not scald his lap with the tea. He leaves with more of my likeness and I try not to imagine where it will end up.

There's no music, tired of songs. Go home and move my bed to a different corner. When things were simpler weren't we two old maiden sister aunts in a hardwood varnished floor apartment, one to knit, one to crochet beads to a backyard picnic table, summer canning berries and peppers and memory. Fine enough even in the mirror above the fireplace where crinkle eyes have lost their suspicion and smugness has gone now with the steady smooth river paddle of routine.

And the scented notepaper reassuringly replies to the girl in her twenties not yet having found her footing that she will. When the sand dries. But it's so hot there is nothing to do but to keep moving.

I waste so much water and chew the inside of my cheeks for proof of teeth. My nails are past the quick and I wish it were a later hour, time for bed. Force a fist through the television, rest with my restless hands, the countdown ticks away seconds as simple as many. They're tearing down all the gargoyles steeples lighthouses. Sky white a little unsteady on its feet. But beauty ain't no liar. Mine is a song and recitation of delectable ungroomed words. Backyards left wild. But I remember how to walk to the passage, old sight complete.

We were just eighteen, in the boot camp since six years old. Certainly able to do more as teenagers but there is always something else of course. Someone snaps. I was sitting upstage in the Russian splits, the sound of tendons just before they tear. I was painting black liquid lines around my eyes. They had to be visible so there would be something else for the patrons to look at if I should fall.

What I thought about last night, my head on a pillow hard as cement, was doing anything to avoid growing into the face of a thirty-five year old bank teller with a peeling French manicure and a ruffle blouse who pops next door every day at lunchtime for a crab salad sandwich and a strawberry Snapple, who if she was pushed out alone on a stage would just giggle from behind her hands.

Eden when did you become so. After all it wasn't so long ago I was ruffly too, patent leather plastic tap shoes. Maybe it's all these orders given in French. Maybe it's the black and pink uniform, maybe it's the local news features with the prime minister watching rehearsals and slouching over the microphone to tell the town to love the country's national sweethearts and become star donors since so much money goes only to sports. A hundred sit ups in a hundred degree room at age ten doesn't seem excessive when there's a brain drain going on.

I no longer think of nothing when I try not to look at myself in the mirror. The place no one wants but which I got stuck with since I came in late and was admonished. I look across the room at Layla who already creaks around arthritic but can't bring herself to tell her thrilled mother. I remember her from back home and her sixth birthday food fight and I don't know what to say to her about it anymore. I think about my adequate for me in the eyes of others but tiresome for me band man boyfriend from highschool normale and how he laughs when Tom Waits says the piano has been drinking not him. How he stumbled over the curb just as my mother passed in the maroon mini van having come in to see me so awake. Sleeping beauty in my sleek bodice that's so tough to breathe in because it's supposed to be painfully difficult but appear to be very easy.

All the girls and the director with their eyeliner tattooed just in case they're ever called upon to take someone's place. Black swan coppelia doll-face to them. It's unspoken yet it seems they probably see it as being no better than that frumpy bank lady.

If I get into med school the first sutures I will ever do will be on an older man with mahogany eyes who'd fallen while chasing after his terrier. He will hum Hank Williams and look down at my feet and ask why I stand with my toes turned out like that. I will say that I was a dancer once and he will say oh he took dance lessons too, at the Arthur Murray school waltzing and tangoing with his wife till his arthritis set in. But they never made him stand like that. I will tell him I was in ballet and he will say he never cared for all that hoity toity crap. "Now Arthur Murray school is stuff you can use. You can dance at weddings without looking like a fool until the young kids go to the DJ and request all that noise. Ballet? Hmph. When would a doctor ever need that? Now ballroom dancing that's something everybody needs. Why my very own daughter was such a wallflower before she got into it. Works at a bank, she's really a lot more confident since she started doing the classes."

The first day of my surgery rotation I will get to choose the music. Flip past Stravinsky and Tchaikovsky for Coltrane and Motown. I'll watch the surgeon place a pin in a young girl's hip and catch myself standing there on feet with ankles forward toes turned back and I turn them in civilian.

It will be hard to get used to at first but I'll feel much more stable on feet set apart parallel. Picture ID next to my heart.

So saintly a child playing at Plato's shadow puppets. Tomorrow's going to be another pop quiz. The tangled skipping rope chalked hopscotch is washed away. Parents' prayers on flashcards with no subtext. But I'll veer off the oval racing track, shock them, not passing the baton off to the next and passing all the rest.

I wear one ill fitting slipper as I taste what is at the bottom of my cup. That wonderful amber heat. Twirl round to become taller, brave, defined white in the light crystal doorknobs, fate and opening it up dreams. I stand at an intersection and double back instead because the crocuses are pushing through the sidewalk cracks. I realize my limp is gone, my hands are not in fists, my jaw is not clenched. Who is coming this way with no memory now of empty pockets minus everything bank account deeds good. And this is the good wealth, the glory untailored.

The best was when it was like a deep lake, buoyant with salt rock muscles, lightness in their resolve and a stretch to time without any kind of drug. Without any repercussions. The worst was how it could be like clawing up a jagged edged mountain, nails being pushed back into their beds, forced to have to grow again, and by the third time around they only grow stub slow. Exhaustion unrewarded. Not a thing admirable in finally getting it right. No praise in finally having learned.

One piece we took a long time to learn. Invisible coconuts in our hands which would hold candles when we got the real ones. Props didn't think to make the edges high enough for the wax not to spill over and we discovered this at first dress rehearsal. The little flames went out, the wax dripped onto the floor and every last one of us slipped and fell on the dark stage. Hope nothing serious. It would keep us from the opening, as if there was any choice. The candle light was supposed to create an ethereal effect but instead we stood in place while the artificial lights were set instead. We thought they set the thermostat too frightfully low on the yearly adjudication day. For some reason six pairs of eyes over pen and paper were more daunting than two hundred or more sitting on winter coats. And now and then the creak opening door of late comers coming in. I gleaned little from the comments in the envelope and realized both sweet and sour grapes come to have the same bland taste.

Grass under my bare smooth feet after the callouses have worn down is as delightful for me as for a child whose first steps are taken in a park with an audience grinning. The constant quest for perfect balance will serve me sometimes sure, but in the end it is better maybe to walk a little off kilter. The Earth often tilts a little and always perfect. I sometimes inexplicably trip over what I thought was something in the way but on the piece of sidewalk there is nothing there.

Now those tacky coconut candle holders are set on the centre of my tea table giving off a little glow. Once in a while I turn them on their side and let the wax spill out. Sometimes there is a pattern but more often I allow for perfect fractal chaos. Although it can be easily scraped off with a fingernail I leave it there and imagine how the surface of the table would be so interesting covered in wax of many colours. A delicate vase would not be able to stand straight of course but it would seem to be at ease that way. It would hold a flower which would bend a little, and bend more still, with the breeze from the open window. Perfect marriage. Some things dance without ever having had to learn.

What shade of white hue of black did the others see in Lord Wall's destitute dented suit of a knight. Who paced in one direction. Clothed in a suzaphone and cymbals to announce your arrival. To those parched souls desperate for any music other than squealing tires, loud garbled bartering, and the echoes and dripping of the sewers not unlike the lead slowly poisoning them. Will not imagine your being completely alone with no one other than the company of bats, vultures, or other wild things not yet found in nature. They lock those fast food chain dumpsters but did you find a way to pry them open and feast on sugary white bread and eight inch canned kind apple pie still hot for a holiday. Was there a West Coast Wall Street where once two dollar bills were replaced with polar bears. The suits were confused and lucky you they tossed what they thought was less. Did you stay in dormitories some nights, in by seven out by morning ten. White bread again possum soup served by well meaning teens with flouride grins extra credit and last story on the news it's a feel good. Were there notebook theories on chemical warfare. Are the Washington boy scouts truly prepared. Did you watch one of the women set out to choose a shopping cart flat only to find them locked up for a quarter she does not have and illiterate to the bylaw warnings for running off with them and the warnings not to run through the supermarket aisles with them below that. Were there really trash can bonfires you were ordered to put out because this part of the country isn't really that cold, or was that just a crime show tactic you laughed at. Watching televisons stacked in the window of the future store. Could a person buy the future in there. Don't pay till 2020. Did they make you go to adult kindergarten to sit and sew potholders for the benefit craft fairs. Did you watch the kids get ancient quick. The rain as oxidizing to their spirits as the cattle and snow lands they left. Did the same officers over and over call you radio situation letter number before they asked your name. Was an Eastside phone booth a direct line to heaven. Were you background for CBC street dramas paid in lunches of box drinks and whipped tuna and mayo on ritz. Photographs can now be poster-sized and high definition yet my imagination sometimes still 1970s half colours in four by six. I know barbed wire on my fence was all along dull enough to not even prick my skin. Yours could have been razor sharp. To get over it you might have stepped down where the bomb was being tested again for the hell of it or it could have been a refuge for rare flowers, the sharps to keep the housewife poachers away. Tea time blossoms for the Wall Street wives, and the bedside apologies for the augumented mistresses. You probably would not have gone to the half-finished condo, safer from bipolar faultlines in the rare doorway without a security gate. You would probably prefer to walk those streets all night and everyone knowing you'd rather not say much but they take comfort in seeing you around every day because even if nothing else changes there is you. And all of them can keep going on. And I can look over my now hunched shoulder and finally say goodbye.

Sugar snow waiting for a different incarnation of winter. I do not know why I am hungry for pinwheel plates of cold cuts and cheeses. Demure in December wearing a dress made for summer nights. House near the country river. When they came over with a box of cider I might find it foolish later I didn't partake. Wouldn't behave as though they knew I was wearing a wire recording. Everything to leave before the bars close. My future self-effacing stand up routine gets me somewhere. What else can I do, it's the night bus, the one without rest stops. The hobo clown at the back with the wine soaked pants. The flat flat land slow rushing by. The engineer won't hide his displeasure. The life the life is riding slick winter rain streets with shoddy shoes wet soil comfort. Wondering about a familiar hare or a cow. So gentle when in their company, almost anyone's company. The averted stares. Precious garments will not distract them from stress. I teeter on my heels flat footed, forced early to arches by picking up pencils with my curled toes and my nails down chalkboard harmony with them. I'm not so far removed and I am someone else too. Forever uncovering discovery in sleep and waking life and at some point it does get blessedly easier.

We have our own author. Words like lather we have and we have insatiable hunger thirst forever. We own our own errors and tricky to own up to what we know we have. We hold iridescent blue orbs, running fingers through the cascades and star dew for more as the sweet quiet holds.

Layla catches me finally opening the book of Blake
she gave me last birthday. Space enough for two on
the moss beneath our older now elm tree. She turns
off the water, comes out to take turns reading.

One makes frail so strong. Bringing Riviera warm and pearl echelon in your Jackie O blacks. No prescription jetting off on a whim voracious. I make myself accustomed to cold and damp rooms. Kicking off the covers. I wore one of those satin pieces to cover my eyes, an oriental pattern and no one ever knew I was not sleeping. I don't wish to see myself as reckless as I am in my dreams otherwise I'd wake up with a million new paths in my head unable to make a choice. I'd hear my own colourful exaggerations and half-way believe them and doubt how capable and thoughtful and worldly I knew myself to truly be. Spending was my analgesic, my fever made to feel cool to anyone who felt my forehead and the clothing fell me so well and I never locked my door at night. Whenever I felt the creeping on my skin I never gave in to the urge to look around and check the low spot on my back for june bugs or baby spiders. I'd kick off my shoes and relish the summer swell of my feet, call up the feeling of my breast stroke and the thin layer of salt on my hair. I never allowed myself to feel persecuted by any question as to how I was doing. My answer became a simple nod and I tried to change the asker's course by guessing correctly as to how they were and was it well and so am I. Loneliness was dismissed with charity used bookstores blooming with high chatter.

There are ways to do so much more than simply get by.

I think it through. I change my mind. It is lovely to be so malleable as the dry street below under winter tires. Doubtful outcome. Spotted windows and the condensation on the sills. Nodding my head to avoid that break apart to be right back to the end where I started. But there is comfort in soft wools and in seeing the house plants come back to life. Everyone checks those double bolts before they turn in and safety reverberates.

What is so strange is the minutes lost and the tastes lost by swallowing too quickly. Making time to turn out the colours and the rhythms that set my feet sturdy on the undulating ground. Making time for lengthy hellos and quick shy goodbyes. I never want to lose it. The slight of hand in the eyes of many will wrap me up in firm understanding.

A holiday is nearing and I catch my breath and lend it back. I remember to look as hundreds of golden chariots whisk me off to where the soil has been turned over and made ready for spring. And the springs beneath do not impede the growing.

Acknowledgements

Heartfelt thanks to: Andy Brown, Garet Markvoort, Bob Hunt, Billy Mavreas, R.D. Roy, Amanda Morse and Dr. Gerald S. Wiviott.

Biscuits and catnip to Benny, Emily, Henry, and Ash.

And most of all, my eternal gratitude and love to Robert and Adrienne Gellman.

Photo by Bob Hunt

Valerie Joy Kalynchuk is a regular contributor to *Matrix* magazine. Her work has also appeared in *Geist, The Original Canadian City Dweller's Almanac, Fish Piss, Career Suicide*, and *You and Your Bright Ideas: New Montreal Writing*. Originally from Winnipeg, she currently lives in Montreal. Her first book was the novella *All Day Breakfast* which was published by conundrum press in 2001.